Parmesan Pig

Charleston, SC
www.PalmettoPublishing.com

Parmesan Pig

First Edition

Hardcover ISBN: 978-1-68515-681-7
Paperback ISBN: 978-1-68515-682-4
eBook ISBN: 978-1-68515-683-1

Copyright: TXu002313982

Parmesan Pig

by Ben Barrowman
illustrated by Alexis Eastburn

To Jane,
A story for your Parmesan Pig
Love, Dad

Every creature on Earth
Has the very same goal,
Thoughts full of joy
And a satisfied soul.

The result is a feeling
That is hard to explain.
You feel it within.
We should give it a name.

Let's all call it HAPPY.
You may have heard it before,
But it's not very simple.
There's a lot to explore.

Some feel it all over
And a lot of the time.
Others feel it is missing
Or a mountain to climb.

But for those that need hope,
There is nothing as big
As the heart of our friend.
Meet Parmesan Pig!

Getting better each year,
Never bitter, just sweet,
With wonderful ingredients,
She is delicious to meet.

Finding more than just food
With the use of her snout,
She can smell when she's needed
To fix a friend's pout.

Let us look at the times
Others needed to hear it.
She helped them with HAPPY
And lifted their spirits.

Her dearest of friends,
Parmesan Pig's favorite dish,
Was Spaghetti Spider,
Who had all you could wish.

He got what he wanted
And could fill a whole plate.
There was plenty of everything,
Even legs...he had eight!

He measured his HAPPY
By counting his toys.
The latest and greatest,
Was a plane that made noise.

6

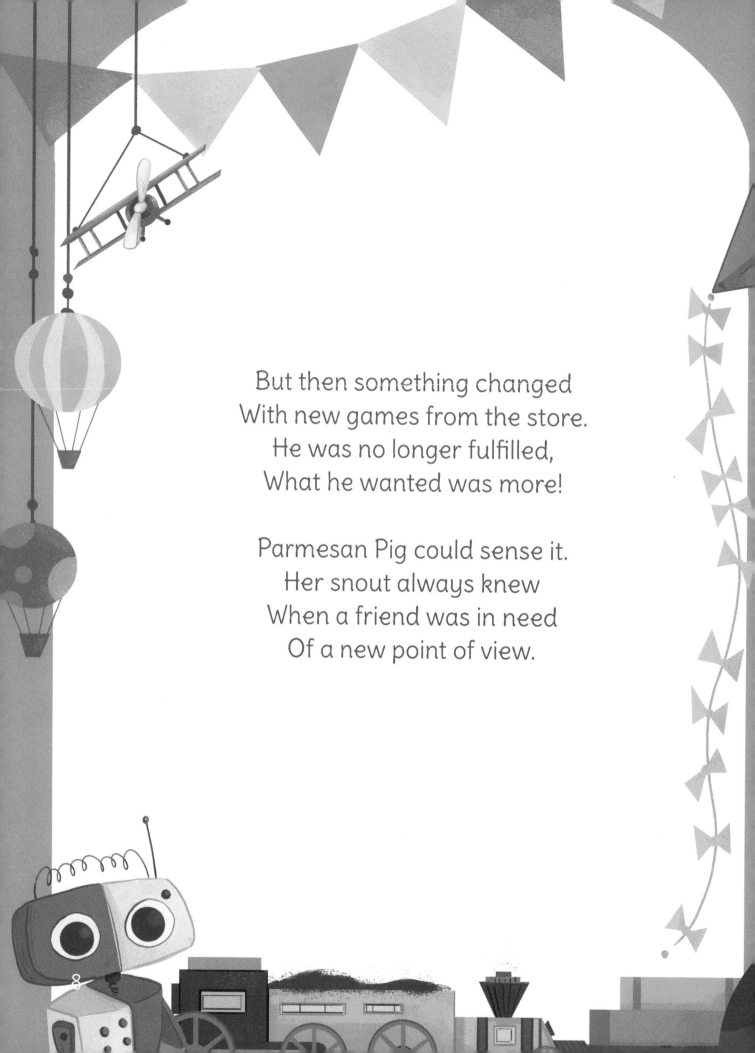

But then something changed
With new games from the store.
He was no longer fulfilled,
What he wanted was more!

Parmesan Pig could sense it.
Her snout always knew
When a friend was in need
Of a new point of view.

She untangled his web
And offered advice,
**"Love what you have
And you won't need it twice."**

**"Do not feel the need
To judge or compare.
You want to be HAPPY?
Take one toy and share."**

She was a friend he could trust.
So, Spaghetti Spider believed
This new way to be HAPPY
Was a web he could weave.

A couple weeks later,
Another uplifting tale,
A slice of support
When feelings were frail.

It had been a whole day
Since Marshmallow Mouse
Felt HAPPY enough
To leave her own house.

Parmesan Pig was mindful
And noticed this trend.
So, she went over to check
On her littlest friend.

For Marshmallow Mouse
It was hard to explain.
She was unsure of herself.
Am I just plain sugar cane?

Her mind wandered and worried.
She did not feel content.
Luckily, Parmesan Pig
Could pick up the scent.

Parmesan Pig offered comfort,
A lot more than most did.
She made a space that was safe
Where no one felt roasted.

She said, **"You are special.
I will help you see how.
You are not just the thoughts
You are having right now."**

**"Let's scurry outside.
We can go for a walk,
Breathe in the fresh air,
And continue to talk."**

Using positive words,
An important life skill,
They made plans for the future
As they walked up a hill.

For Marshmallow Mouse,
Who was stuck in a trap,
Parmesan Pig was the friend
Who was there in a snap.

This next story is different.
It's about moving forward,
Helping her friend Taco Turtle,
Whom she really adored.

He was usually HAPPY
And not one to frown,
But life is not fair,
It can flip upside down.

Some recent events,
For Taco Turtle were hard.
He had to work through it,
So Parmesan Pig wrote him a card.

I care so so much,
About how you feel.
I am here and will listen
While you let your heart heal.

You are not feeling HAPPY.
It doesn't feel there at all.
But while you feel sad,
Please keep your head tall.

Soon, wiggle your tail.
Let it out of the shell.
And when you are ready,
Ring your own bell.

Then flip and roll over.
And no matter how slow,
Start moving forward
Wherever you go.

As time will go on,
Believe what I say.
You may find that HAPPY
Will find you on the way.

Your friend,
Parmesan Pig

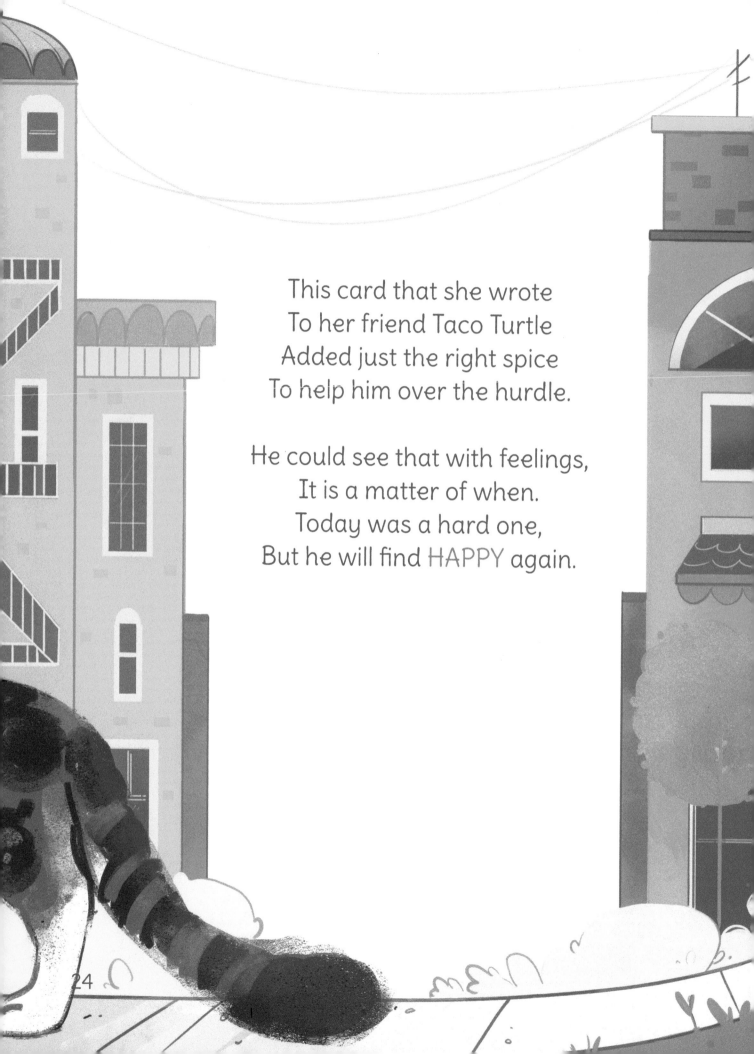

This card that she wrote
To her friend Taco Turtle
Added just the right spice
To help him over the hurdle.

He could see that with feelings,
It is a matter of when.
Today was a hard one,
But he will find HAPPY again.

Parmesan Pig knows that HAPPY
Can be something we chase,
But if you catch it just right
It is hard to erase.

These next friends of hers
Love life for the sake of it.
In all situations,
You get what you make of it.

There is Celery Swan,
Who cannot carry a tune,
Yet sings in the pond
From morning 'til moon.

Or for those that feel stress,
Like Watermelon Whale,
She has learned to take breaks.
You should see her exhale!

Some friends often feel sick,
Like Sir Pepper Leopard,
Yet, he finds joy in his life.
His strength should be treasured.

And last but not least
Is Pineapple Parrot,
Who knows only one word,
But is **"HAPPY"** to share it!

HAPPINESS is a mystery.
It can be a bit strange.
It comes and it goes.
There is quite a range.

When seeking out HAPPY,
To improve your chance,
Eat healthy foods,
Exercise, even dance!

Whatever you are,
Let it all out.
Be around others
Who don't make you doubt.

And don't be afraid
To let out a snort.
Like Parmesan Pig,
Roll out your support.

We want for our loved ones,
Every neighbor and friend,
To be blessed with HAPPY
Without any pretend.

Parmesan Pig always knows,
With the right frame of mind,
She will mostly feel HAPPY
A big chunk of the time.

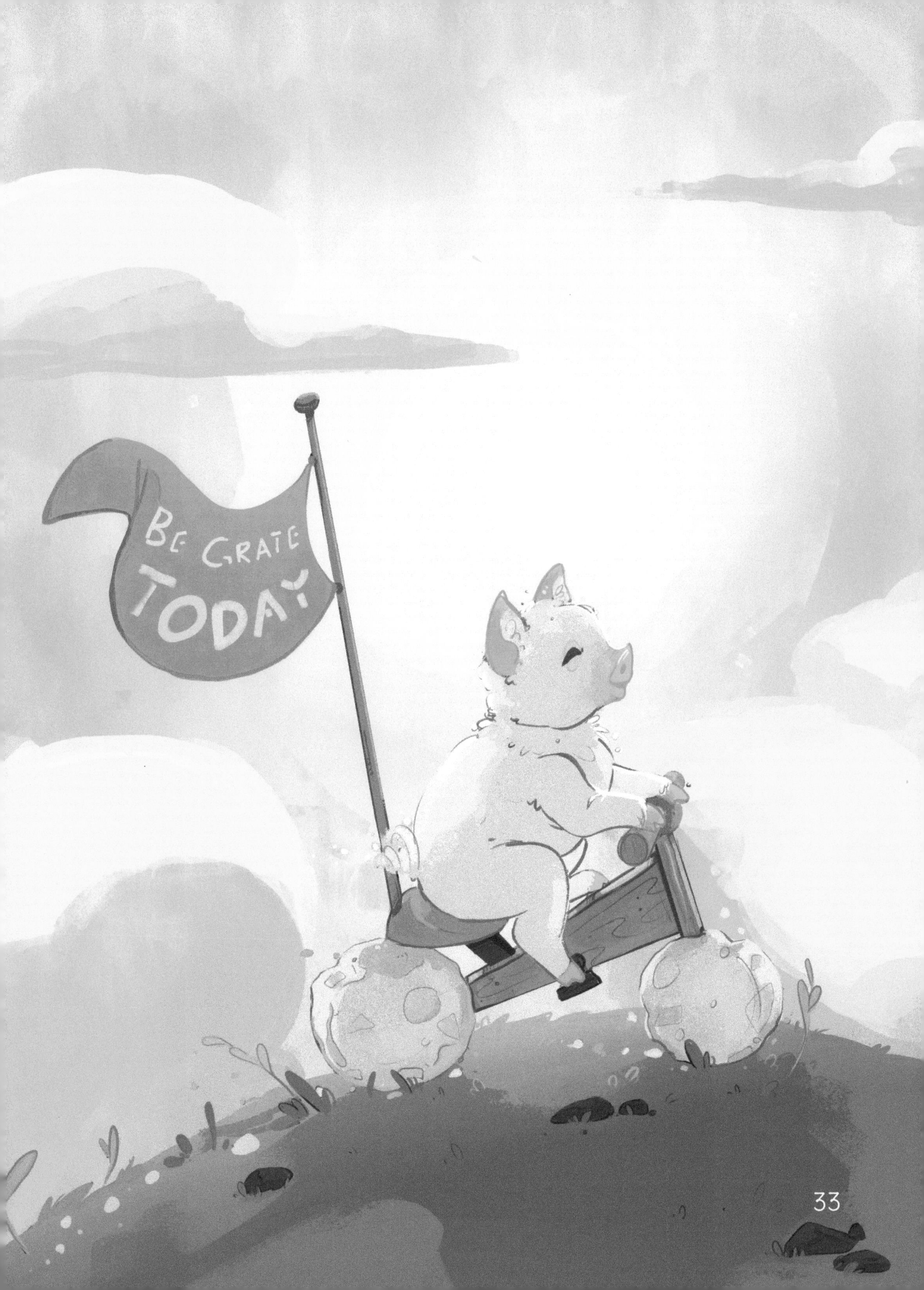
BE GRATE
TODAY

About the Author

Ben Barrowman has a passion for creative rhythmic storytelling that helps children understand the importance of supporting one another. He enjoys summer vacations on Goose Rocks Beach in Maine with his wife Lauren, and two children, Connor and Jane. It was there with his family that the characters in this story were imagined.

CPSIA information can be obtained
at www.ICGtesting.com
Printed in the USA
JSHW060812050223
37164JS00007B/66